Otto Stechhan

Rudder, Rod and Gun
Poems of Nature

ISBN/EAN: 9783337021832

Printed in Europe, USA, Canada, Australia, Japan

Cover: Foto ©Andreas Hilbeck / pixelio.de

More available books at **www.hansebooks.com**

Otto Stechhan

Rudder, Rod and Gun

Poems of Nature

POE E

CAR

CONTENTS.

"In wood and field, by lake and stream
I love to linger and to dream."

THE above sentiment has, in a great measure, been responsible for the poems contained in this little volume, all of them expressions of the instincts of the true sportsman who finds both pleasure and compensation in his quest for game, regardless of consideration for his "bag" being satisfied, no matter how unsuccessful in that direction, with whatever nature so lavishly, in a thousand other ways, proffers him in his rambles in forest and in field, and his voyages on lake and stream.

The sportsman's intimate knowledge of out-door life, of the habits of the game which he seeks, the natural phenomena incidental to the weather and to the seasons, give him a wide scope of information, attained by no other occupation, at once instructive as well as entertaining, not appreciated however by those not endowed with the instinct which urges him to roam in nature's fair domain.

The sportsman, as a rule, is not accredited with a poetic soul, owing possibly to his association with death-dealing instruments, and to his general "matter-of-fact" methods, or possibly due also to the

3

absence of literature, poetic in sentiment, expressive of his appreciation for the grand and beautiful in nature, referring particularly to the favorite haunts of game, for which he manifests the greatest interest. His established reputation for fabrication (vivid imagination) brought to an ideal conception should, however, lead to other conclusions, unfortunately not yet realized. Be that as it may, I am convinced that the word paintings illustrative of the "sportsman's paradise" contained herein will touch a responsive chord in his bosom which possibly only lacks the power of expression to make his own harp ring out joyfully in unison to my own, for deep down in the heart of every genuine sportsman a kindred feeling lingers, sympathetic and tender, which, though it may lie dormant, is ready to be kindled into a lucid flame when brought into contact with voicings so familiar, so endeared to his inmost heart and soul.

OTTO STECHHAN.

RETURN TO NATURE.

O, GIVE me life, unfettered, free,
  In wood and field, on land and sea,
On surging river, bounding main,
On mountains high, on grassy plain;
There let me go, rejoiced, content
In wilderness to strike my tent.
Where nature revels on its throne,
Untrammeled reigns, supreme, alone,
There let me rove, exultant, free,
My soul attuned in harmony
To what so grandly, what so proud,
In accents sweet, in voicings loud,
Speaks volumes to my yearning soul,
And beacons me to freedom's goal.

O, give me life, unfettered, free,
Where I the vaulted heaven see;
Where I the birth of day and night,
The storm can view in all its might;
Where unobstructed is my view,
And habitations are but few;

5

Where zephyrs utter sermons grand,
The ocean beats upon the strand.
To sylvan glens, with flowers strewn,
To mount and cliff, by nature hewn,
Far from the wiles of cunning man
Removed from his refining ban ;
There let me roam, O grant the boon—
With nature, there let me commune.

MY DOG AND I.

MY gun in hand, the eye alert,
   My faithful dog in sight,
O'er wood and field, I gayly roam
  In rapturous delight.
On grasses gray, the frost is seen
  On stubblefield and corn;
And scattered lie the rustling leaves
  From bush and branches shorn.
The air is crisp, a hawk perhaps
  Is soaring in the sky;
And cawing crows on forage bent
  Pass slowly flying by.
Through shocks of corn new wheat is seen,
  Each shock a toiler's crown;
The barren trees look ghostly now,
  The weeds are broken down.
The woodbine and the sumac yet
  Their crimson banners fly;
And often yet a violet
  Belated, greets mine eye.

7

A fragrance sweet, from bog and marsh,
  Comes wafting through the air,
Far sweeter than from mignonette
  Combined with roses fair.
And beating thus through wood and dale
  Expectant up and down,
A thousand wonders do I find
  In wood and stubble brown.
When suddenly, as if transformed,
  My dog, where leaves are strewn,
Points, head erect, a picture grand
  As if from marble hewn.
"To ho! To ho!" my canine friend,
  I warning lift the hand;
The blood leaps tingling in my veins
  As I expectant stand,
My dog admiring, proud and stanch—
  Then flush the hiding quail;
Pick off a bird, perhaps a pair,
  As to the wood they sail.
And so the day with nature spent
  On hillside and in dale,
I take delight, my dog and I—
  To seek the fleeting quail.

AWAY, AWAY.

AWAY, away from musty room,
  From toil, and chase for gain;
Let troubles all and care behind,
  Let nature thee ordain.

Away, away, the bluebird calls
  From morn till fades the day;
The robin sings, the medowlark,
  This gladsome roundelay.

Away, away, to hill and dell,
  To meadows green and fair,
To brook and stream, to murm'ring spring
  Where balmy is the air.

Away, to woods, to shady nooks
  Where flowers thee invite,
To where in every blade of grass
  Is pictured new delight.

Away, away, to azure skies,
  To clouds enshrined in gold,
To where thine eyes in blissful dream
  A paradise behold.

9

Away, away, to fertile fields
    That promise golden grain,
To where the bells of lowing herds
    Contentedness proclaim.

Away to where thy happy song
    A joyous echo wakes,
Where mirth abides, where joy presides,
    New lease thy life partakes.

FLY FISHING.

OH, the grandeur of the glist'ning stream,
   As it winds its joyous way,
A torrent of silver, by gold enshrined
   When in glory awakens the day.
How it bubbles and babbles in mirthful play,
   O'erleaping the rock with a bound,
Incessantly murm'ring in accents of glee,
   Yet in language majestic, profound.
How graceful it passes the verdure-clad shore,
   And smiles where the flowers appear,
Tempestuous then rushes in leaps and in bounds
   To the cataract, roaring anear.

'Tis the stream which the angler expectantly seeks
   With his rod and his gay colored fly,
At early morn, or at eventide,
   When propitious is smiling the sky.
He noiselessly wades the crystalline flood,
   Where the ripples so merrily pass,
While seeking the haunts where the trout congre-
     gate,
   Or the monarch of waters, the bass.

11

With well-poised hand he drops his fly,
  So tempting and so bright,
Where a whirling pool to a strike invites,
  A sight for the angler's delight.
And he skips his lure, to nature true,
  And it dances on the sheen ;
When suddenly the waters break
  And the king of the fishes is seen
As he grabs the fly with a vicious bound,
  Then the angler lets him lead
Against the current's surging might,
  When he strikes, and checks his speed.

For a moment only, he slacks his pace,
  The fish now hooked secure,
When again he speeds to the rocks away
  In the hope of disgorging the lure.
But the angler has him well in hand
  With his pliant, whip-like rod ;
And he lets him run, then reels him in
  With a smile, an approving nod.
Then vainly endeavors the wily fish
  As he leaps the waters clear,
To part the line, to flee the barb,
  As away he darts, in fear.

Unequal the battle, the angler's skill
    Full oft does not avail;
For the cunning fish will break his bonds
    (An oft-repeated tale).
But when the angler wins the fray,
    And he reels his treasure in,
That strains the line with angry might
    With barb-extended fin;
Then ask in vain for a grander sight
    This battle, the final to see,
The defiant eye of the struggling fish
    As in vain he endeavors to flee.

His prize secure and flushed with pride,
    Again he whips the stream,
Expectantly, from shore to shore,
    And his eyes with pleasure gleam.

MAXINKUCKEE.

MAXINKUCKEE, glist'ning water,
    Where tradition weaves a chain
'Round the red man's earthly heaven,
    Aubeenaubee's fair domain.
Thou, O precious crystal fountain,
    So enchanting, dazzling, fair,
Thou reflecting, sparkling water,
    As translucent as the air ;
Thee I cherish as a treasure
    Of a song, a sweet refrain,
Brightest jewel 'mong the treasures
    Which in mem'ry I retain.

Like a diamond set in em'ralds
    Vieing with the orb of day,
'Tween the woodland, in the valley,
    Where the sunbeams dance and play,
Where the turtle-dove, the robin,
    Build their nests within thy sight,
And the lark her songs is warbling,
    Carols of supreme delight.

14

On the meadows near thee roaming,
 Lowing herds I browsing trace,
And a streamlet, silver flowing,
 Bounding, leaps in thy embrace.
Lilies, mirrored in thy splendor,
 Nod their heads, immaculate,
And their fragrance so enticing
 Dreams of fairyland create.
Sails are on thy bosom plying,
 Pinioned birds of graceful mold,
And the seagulls, 'round thee hov'ring,
 Lazily, their wings unfold.
Maidens fair, the oars are plying,
 Paddling the frail canoe,
And the sailors, storm defying,
 Crafty, steer the billows through.
'Tis a picture ne'er forgotten,
 Tranquilly it comes to view,
Heaven's mirage on the waters
 Forms a boundless vault of blue.
Indiana, proud, distinguished,
 Wear this jewel of renown,
Fairest gem of all thy treasures,
 Wear it proudly in thy crown.
Maxinkuckee, glist'ning water,
 Where tradition weaves a chain
'Round the red man's earthly heaven,
 Aubeenaubee's fair domain.

YACHTING.

WHITE fleeting clouds the sky adorn,
  And balmy is the air.
The glistening sun and dancing waves
  Proclaim the wind is fair.
The anchored yacht, like a tethered hound,
  When the bugle call is heard
When the chase is on, strains at her chain;
  Then the captain gives the word.
"All hands on deck! the mainsail hoist!
  The halyards, quick, belay!
The anchor heave! haul up the jib!"
  We're off! we sail away!
To the breezes float the streamers gay,
  The "Union Jack" on high;
The sails are full, and we speed along
  In ecstacies of joy.
To the Wind she heels, his winning ways,
  To his wooing well inclined;
The waves caress her glist'ning prow,
  Fair rivals of the Wind.

The rudder grasped with steady hand,
  She glides the waters proud.
A thing of life she seems to me,
  Responsive, sheet and shroud.

The swallows dart from azure sky,
  Skip o'er the water light;
The seagull passes slowly by
  In ever-changing flight.
Oh, give to me on waters wide
  With shores by nature blest,
Where skies are blue, the wind is fair,
  A yacht, by winds caressed.
A buoyant steed, with pinions spread,
  With boon companions gay,
The rudder give to me in hand,
  Then would I sail away;
And glide upon the crested wave
  With troubles all alee;
Not care I for a vested crown,
  Sail I the waters free.

IN THE BOOK OF NATURE.

NOT on parchment, or Papyrus,
   Stained and tattered, gray with age,
Not in volumes, books imposing,
   Illustrated page by page,
Would I read what guides the planets,
   Why the day must follow night,
Who the glorious sky has painted,
   Where the sun obtains his light,
How the woodland was created,
   Who directs the storm, the winds,
How the mountain high was builded,
   And the stream the ocean finds,
Who to birds their song has given,
   Beauteous dress to flowers fair,
Clad in verdure field and meadow,
   Life created everywhere.

At another fount I tarry,
   Flowing ever, pure and rare;
What I seek, I there discover
   In the book of Nature, fair.

And the leaves, enraptured turning,
   All absorb'ed, deep, intent,
Blissfully the lines perusing,
   Seek I knowledge and content.
Truth I find here, not conjectures,
   Monuments I here exhume;
Why should questions, here, I proffer—
   "Why exhales the rose perfume?"
And I study not, and ponder,
   Neither weigh I here nor there,
But accept the blessings offered
   As assign'ed to my share.

Nature's ways, impenetrable,
   Infinite, none can divine,
What she offers thee, implicit,
   Oh, accept it,—it is thine.

HUNTING THE PHEASANT.

WHERE the jackoak thrives and the
    papaw grows,
The black haw, and the red,
Where densely grows the underbrush,
   In leaf strewn mossy bed,
Where prickly thorns and elders rank
   Combine to balk our way,
The roses wild in clusters grow
   And squirrel and chipmunk play,
Where silver springs come babbling on
   ' Tween ridges domiciled;
There goes the hunter, sport intent
   To seek the pheasant, wild.

He silently pursues his way,
   The faithful dog ahead,
Where tangled vines the brush entwine,
   The berry branches, red;
And following till drumming sound
   Afar has caught his ear,
Expectant now his gun in hand,
   He slowly draws anear.

Where cautiously the trailing dog
  Creeps patiently in sight,
And suddenly stands, head erect,
  A picture of delight.
Now unobserved the hunter spies,
  Still drumming, proud, sedate,
The gorgeous plumaged wily bird,
  Oblivious to its fate,
On mossy log, with flutt'ring wings,
  Where emanates the sound,
With crested neck, sedate and proud,
  As if by magic, bound.
The sportsman's instinct true prevails,
  He'll not improve his chance,
He flush's the bird, and off it sails
  Awakened from its trance.
Now caring well to place the trees
  Between the danger line,
Sagacity, experience
  Here, readily combine.
With pinions spread, with lightning speed,
  With startling, whirring sound,
Now straight away, alarmed, it flies
  And skims the verdant ground.
The ready gun now speaks aloud,
  We trust it spoke in vain;
And lost to view, the bird sails on
  And the Hunter tries again.

Perhaps he bags a bird or two,
    He fully feels repaid;
The fragrant wood, the pheasant's call,
    The thousand charms displayed,
Are compensation hundredfold
    For fruitful hours spent
In forest wild, in solitude,
    Fair haven of content.

WAWASEE.

WAWASEE! Wawasee!
    Haven of tranquillity.
Nature pure, yet undefiled,
Claims this jewel, fair and wild,
With its waters wind-caressed,
Shores with wood and verdure blessed.
Where the skies of azure blue, ;
Mirrored, come again to view,
Winged steeds thy bosom ply,
Proudly go careening by.

Wawasee! Wawasee!
Where the hours enchanting flee,
Balmy zephyrs breathe delight,
Care and troubles take to flight,
Merriment yet reigns supreme
In a constant, joyous stream.
Where the sailors, brave and bold,
Like the errant knights of old,
Fly their colors to the air,
Tokens from their ladies fair.

Wawasee! Wawasee!
In my dreams, thou'rt haunting me.
Stretching out thy glit'ring sheen
Far through field and valley green—
Where the crane sedately flies,
And the loon so plaintive cries;
Fishes sport in merry play,
Throwing off a silver spray;
And the redwing's song of cheer
Brings sweet music to mine ear.

Wawasee! Wawasee!
Harken to the melody,
Of its wavelets rippling on,
Singing their bewitching song,
Of its waters ever bright,
Bringing to our soul delight.
Fresh'ning breezes, azure skies,
Longings sweet, and laughing eyes,
Murm'rings thus, are greeting thee;
Welcome all, to Wawasee.

RETURNING TO CAMP.

DENSE silence reigns on the prairie marsh;
 I leave the shelt'ring blind,
For the flight has ceased, and I push my way
 To the river, near, defined.
The sun has set, and weirdly formed,
 The barren trees are seen
That fringe the shore of the winding stream,
 The sycamore between,
That stretches out its ghostly arms,
 Now creaking in the wind,
That blows a gale, a wintry wail,
 As the trail I labored find.

I stand erect, astern my boat,
 The pliant paddle, aside,
And I guide it well, and I steer my course,
 As I skim the waters wide.
In the bow, are heaped the mallard duck,
 The pintail and the teal;
The ready gun and the sleeping dog,
 The grass in the boat conceal.

In love am I with my light bateau,
  So graceful, slender, strong,
A buoyant steed, a thoroughbred,
  It glides the stream along.
I feel a king of this vast domain,
  And I know my subjects all,
Inhabiting the wood, the marsh,
  And they harken to my call.

I float adown the darksome flood,
  So treacherous, so deep;
And I feel my way, for the night is dark,
  And a watchful vigil keep,
Till a beacon light, from the distance bright,
  The camp brings to my view,
Where I land my boat and its precious load,
  And long for the flight anew.

THE SPORTSMAN TRUE.

'TIS not the quest for game alone
    Which urges me to go,
To wood and field, on sport intent,
    Where rippling waters flow.
'Tis to commune with nature grand,
In freedom's realms to roam,
    To view the morn at break of day,
The woodland in the gloam;
To harken to the song bird's lay,
    Its wild, enchanting air,
To view the leaf, the garnered sheaf,
    The flowers wild, the fair;
The cataract, to see descend
    The glist'ning crystal run,
To mirrored view the waters clear,
    The skies, the verdant shore;
To see the waves dash on the beach
    To listen to their roar,
To breathe the air, so pure so rare,
    The odor of the wood,
Rejuvenating heart and soul
    In precious solitude.

A thousand charms hath wood and dale,
  A thousand tongues that speak,
Revealing to mine inmost soul,
  What blissfully I seek.
O solitude, in woodland, wild,
  By thee O nature true,
Their inspirations, hopes, desires,
  Anew, my soul imbue.
And bag I feather not, nor fin,
  True happiness is mine,
For blissfully the day was spent
  With reveries divine.
'Tis not the quest for game alone
  Which urges me to go,
To wood and field, on sport intent,
  Where rippling waters flow.
'Tis to commune with nature grand,
  In freedom's realms to roam,
To view the morn, the starry night,
  The wildwood in the gloam.

THE FISHERMAN.

THE new-born day has just appeared,
    The slumb'ring earth to greet;
The placid lake lies dreaming yet,
    Translucent at my feet.
I push my boat, the fish to lure
    Into the crystal sheen,
And silently I dip the oars
    Which in the sunlight gleam.
Light ripples follow in the wake
    And spread in circles wide,
Like smiles upon a dimpled face
    They o'er the water glide.
In splendor beams the verdant shore,
    Where songbirds sing their lay,
And blossoms white, and tender green,
    Proclaim the reign of May.
Gold-tinted clouds adorn the sky,
    Which mirrored come to view,
Till lake and sky appear as one,
    A boundless vault of blue.

A plaintive cry comes from afar,
  A loon calls to its mate,
Kingfishers chat'ring seek their prey,
  High flies the crane, sedate.
Then suddenly the clicking reel
  Disturbs my reverie;
And striking quickly, rod in hand,
  The line now running free,
I play the bass, the royal game,
  The king of fishes all,
Who tries in vain his doom to flee,
  His folly to recall.
In vain he leaps into the air,
  His eyes in anger burn,
Then darts away with lightning speed,
  But promptly to return.
He tries again, in vain he leaps
  The cruel barb to flee;
With pliant rod I hold him well
  And bring him soon alee.
And when the battle's fairly won,
  My blood yet coursing high,
My prize I view in glad surprise,
  A sight for gods to spy.
Then doubly blest seems life again,
  The sky a brighter hue,
And joyfully continuing
  I cast my line anew.

IN THE MARSH.

WHERE the sawgrass sharp, the cattail tall,
 The wild rice thickly grows,
Where lily-pads sway in the breeze,
 And slow the water flows;

Where muskrats build their houses quaint,
 A grass entangled mound,
Where the buckthorn and the willow tree
 In copses thick, abound;

To prairie waste, to bottom land
 Submerged by overflow,
Where scrub-oaks fringe the shore along,
 Expectantly I go.

There hiding snugly in my boat,
 Concealed by grasses high,
I vigil keep, my gun in hand,
 And eager scan the sky.

I hear the redwing's joyous song,
 I watch the crane sedate,
Kingfishers darting for their prey,
 As for the flight I wait.

Near, my decoys bob up and down,
    My calls, deception bring;
The ducks attracted crane their necks,
    Sail down with rigid wing.

Now speaks the gun in double tone,
    Profuse the feathers fly,
And here and there, upon their backs
    Now prone the beauties lie.

And so from morn till comes the night
    From out the grassy blind,
By luring on the waterfowl,
    I recreation find.

And when at last, though loath to go,
    I homeward push my way,
Though weary, yet refreshed in mind,
    I praise the glorious day.

While resting then, in ease, at home,
    In mind, the flight I see,
I scan the marsh, the sky afar,
    In meditative glee.

CANOEING.

IKE a fairy craft, so airy, light,
  Like a swan that rides the sea,
So graceful, silent, beautiful,
  In sweet tranquillity;
So glides my boat, my bark canoe,
  Adown the silver stream,
And speeds along majestical,
  Triumphant, proud, serene.
The paddle breaks the glist'ning sheen
  And drips with liquid gold;
Scarce ruff'ling the waters, the surface fair,
  In the wake not a wave we behold.
She rides the sea, she braves the storm,
  My graceful, light canoe;
Secure I feel from wind and storm
  And I live my life anew,
For I breathe the air at nature's fount,
  Its beauty all, I view;
The verdant shore, the azure sky,
  My soul with awe imbue.

And reverently, I cease to ply
　　The paddle's dext'rous might,
As zephyrs waft my boat along
　　In fanciful delight.
Oh, could I thus my buoyant steed
　　With thee, though light and frail,
But staunch and true, adown the stream
　　Of time, forever sail,
With blithesome heart, observingly
　　The world, the fair, to see,
With eye alert, my course defined,
　　With troubles vanished, free ;
Then drifting down the stream of life
　　Rejoiced, merrily,
I'd sing my song, and paddle on
　　In blissful reverie.

THE DEER HUNT.

WHERE the pine tree rears his giant head,
  Where cypress, cedars grow,
Palmettoes on the hummocks thrive,
  And springs of silver flow;
Where white the soil as fallen snow
  Contrasts with vivid green,
And clinging vines the trees adorn
  With trailing moss between;
Where dwells the woodman in his tent,
  And custom yet is law,
Where nature reigns, untrammeled, wild,
  In sunkissed Florida;
There seeks the hunter, gun in hand,
  To find the fleeting deer,
And stealthily he scans the ground
  Where tracks to view appear.
For signs, yet fresh, to trail upon,
  Which promise rich reward,
And patiently he follows on
  The hound now trailing hard.

Until by the waters hid from view
  By grasses thick and tall,
The dog strikes up familiar sounds—
  (The hunter's bugle call).
His blood is up, and runs apace
  Like lava in his veins;
His ready gun is quickly poised
  But patience him retains.
For madly bounding through the wood
  The startled deer appears,
His antlers thrown upon his back
  As through the brush he tears.
His eyes like balls of fire gleam,
  As bounding he goes by,
A picture fair, no mortal ken
  Could fairer ever spy.
The baying hound is on his heels,
  He strides the forest proud,
When echoes through the silent wood
  The hunter's gun aloud.
On speeds the deer, as if the lead
  Had missed its royal goal,
But conscious of his trusted gun
  So well in his control,
He follows in the trail again,
  A crimson dotted way,
The telltale of the hunter's aim
  Which never leads estray.

The monarch of the wood is found
  In death still showing pride,
And watching o'er his trophy grand,
  The winded hound beside.
Praise not to me the crowns of fame,
  The rapturous delight,
By honors and ambition wrought,
  By mammon's purchased might.
Praise not to me the sights of Rome,
  Of ancient Palestine,
The wonders of a fairy land,
  A paradise sublime.
But give to me the royal sport,
  To memory so dear;
The gun's report, the baying hound
  Is music to mine ear.
O let me roam in forests wild,
  Give me a gun, a hound,
Not care I then for pelf or gain,
  My paradise is found.

HUNTING THE SNIPE.

'TIS early morn, the rain has ceased—
    An ideal April day;
The ground is wet, the air is warm,
    The sun yet far away.
Before me spreads the silent marsh,
    A streamlet runs between,
The budding wood appears afar
    In varied tints of green.
A straggling duck is in the sky,
    The plover skims the ground;
From jaokoak copse comes merrily
    The pheasant's drumming sound.
On blackened soil, by fire charred,
    A treacherous morass,
Appear in spots of tender green
    New shoots of virgin grass.
My gun well poised, I stroll along,
    And wade the water slow,
To where a bubbling spring invites
    Where tangled grasses grow;

Where the bucklebrush and the willow thrives,
    The croaking frog is heard,
There would I seek, on sport intent,
    The snipe, the kingly bird.
And suddenly in zig-zag flight,
    Intoning notes of fear,
"Escape! Escape!" familiar sound
    Comes joyous to mine ear.
The trusted gun speaks once or twice,
    Oft' at a distance great,
For quickly scents the wily bird
    The danger and its fate.
"Escape! Escape!" again is heard,
    The gun resents the cry,
And quick reports the echoes wake
    As up the beauties fly.
And many a bird that gave alarm,
    No more will sound the note,
The trophies in the hunter's bag
    His steady aim denote.
The sun in all its glory now
    Ascending to the sky,
Gives zest anew unto the sport,
    The flying birds to spy;
And watching closely where they light,
    A task too oft in vain,
We beat the marsh, both up and down,
    To flush the birds again—

Until at last the sun has set,
   The day of sport is spent,
A true respite from strife and toil,
   A day of rare content.
And when at ease at home again,
   "Escape," the warning note,
The zig-zag flight of startled snipe,
   Still in my vision float.

CAMPING ON THE KANKAKEE.

MY boat is beached, my tent is pitched
    Where shelt'ring trees abound,
On gentle slope, by waters fair,
    On verdure covered ground,
Where silently the Kankakee,
    From marsh and prairie fed,
Mysteriously his winding way,
    Pursues in mossy bed.
Where garlands green, across the stream
    Extend from tree to tree,
The grape entwines the ivy vine,
    The woodbine, fair to see;
Where undefiled by human wiles
    Reigns nature, yet—supreme;
There, dreaming in my cozy tent,
    I view the murm'ring stream.
The finny tribe I see disport
    In ever restless throng;
The waterfowl on play intent,
    And list the starling's song.

And when the evening's shadows fall
  The bird has sought its nest,
The hooting owl alone is heard,
  All nature seems at rest;
Then o'er the camp, the fire bright
  Spreads magic light around,
Gigantic shadows, weirdly formed,
  Across the waters bound.
The flaring light, the darkness dense,
  The stillness of the night,
To reveries grand, eloquent,
  My yearning soul invite.
Content I feel, the world is mine,
  I soar on pinions free,
With nature I commune again
  In blissful harmony.
And from the embers burning low,
  Now far into the night,
As through the boughs the zephyrs sigh,
  The stars appear to sight;
A vision fair comes to my view,
  A maiden pure, divine,
And longingly, my heart aglow,
  Speaks out, "O maiden fair.
Be thou the queen of this domain,
  With me this kingdom share.

Then hand in hand, I'll roam with thee,
In song thy reign proclaim;
Remov'ed from the haunts of man,
Untrammeled by his chain,
In the sunshine of our love we'll bask,
Breathe freedom's balmy air,
We'll float adown the beauteous stream,
From troubles free, and care.
The wood will be our castle grand,
Our blessed, happy home;
Our cot shall be a mossy bank,
Our roof the azure dome.
Oh, couldst thou read my soul aright,
The inspiration feel,
Which beckons me at nature's throne
In ecstasy to kneel;
Then gladly wouldst thou share with me
My home, beside the stream,
And joyfully the days would flee,
A blissful, happy dream."

A CHILD AGAIN.

I CLOSE mine eyes, for the day is gone,
   In woodland spent, in field,
Where worshiping at nature's shrine,
   A heaven was revealed.
And reveries of halcyon days,
   Of woodland fair and wild,
Come back to me where oft I roamed,
   A joyous happy child.
Again I am the careless boy,
   Of fanciful desire,
By name I call my playmates all,
   Like I, in brief attire.
The melon patch upon the hill
   Distinctly comes to view,
The stolen fruit (I taste it still),
   None sweeter ever grew
The logfires near the pasture bright,
   An Indian I, in mind,
The stories told within its glare
   Responsive echo find.

44

The orchards all, which I had known,
  The apples (never ripe),
The peaches in our neighbor's yard,
  Appear again to sight.
The pond, a lake of magnitude,
  Which often I explored
In quest of fish, the nimble frog,
  My boat, a single board.
The chipmunk and the flying squirrel,
  Their antics in the wood
I watch again, and list the song
  Of birds I understood.
The swimming hole, the log across
  The sandbar where we played,
When not disporting in the flood
  From home, from school estrayed.
The haunted house, inspiring awe,
  Where spirits found abode,
Comes as of yore again to view,
  And wide, I shun the road.

O memory of childhood days,
  When all the world was fair,
When earth was yet a paradise
  And I was free from care,
Sweet reveries of halcyon days,
  I could be reconciled,
Again to be a romping boy,
  In thought, in deed, a child.

TENTING.

NEAR a crystal stream in a virgin wood,
  Where whisp'ring zephyrs sigh
Through shelt'ring boughs and drooping vines,
  And echoes find reply;
There on some knoll, commanding view,
  I build a castle grand,
I strike my tent, so airy, light,
  Ingeniously planned.
A fascination ne'er explained,
  Possession takes of me,
As monarch of this fair estate,
  Its quaint simplicity,
I feel a freeman once again
  To wield the ax, the keen,
The open sky above to see,
  Around the verdant green.
To listen to the babbling stream—
  ‧ The songbird's carols fair,
The echo which the ax awakes,
  Clear sounding through the air.

From fragrant leaves my bed is made,
   Well spread upon the ground,
Within my tent, a downy couch,
   None better can be found.
My meals are simple, but suffice,
   Prepared in vessels few,
But relished more than banquet feast
   With all its dazzling hue.
The camp-fire's weird, enchanting glare,
   Built near a fallen tree,
Its crackling noise, the lucid flames,
   Adduce to reverie.
And whate'er good, and whate'er grand
   Is slumb'ring in thy breast,
Communing here at nature's shrine,
   With life-inspiring zest,
A better man 'twill make of thee,
   More patient, more benign,
Life's battles will less irksome be,
   The sun will fairer shine;
The shadows which will cross thy path
   So dark will never be,
But that thou canst them penetrate,
   Afar, the dawning see.
Refreshed at this virgin fount,
   Whilst camping in thy tent,
The fire bright, the open sky,
   Will bring thee rare content.